Copyright © 2023 by Elizabella Baker All rights reserved.

No part of this work may be used, stored, reproduced, or transmitted without written permission from the author except for brief quotations for review purposes as permitted by the law.

The characters and events portrayed in this book are fictitious. Any similarity to real persons, living or dead, is coincidental and not intended by the author.

Editor: Raechelle Downing

Proofreader: Judy Zweifel, Judy's Proofreading

Cover Design ©KiWi Cover Design Co.

Paperback ISBN: 9798859507160

Printed in the United States of America

 Created with Vellum

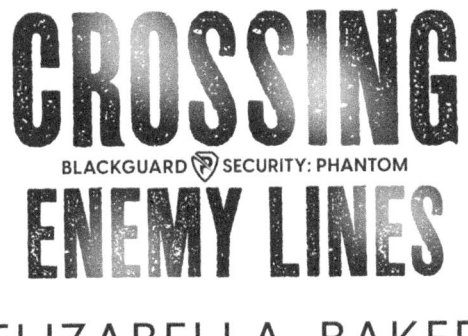

CROSSING ENEMY LINES

BLACKGUARD SECURITY: PHANTOM

ELIZABELLA BAKER

CHAPTER ONE

Daniel looked through his binoculars at the villa down below. The place would probably be considered beautiful if it wasn't owned by a murderer. However, the security was shit. An open door on the balcony gave him the perfect shot to take his target out and walk away. One pull of the trigger and it would all be over, if he so chose.

"Do you ever plan to tell us who our target is?" Gage's question came through his comm.

He couldn't keep the information to himself for much longer. Daniel was surprised they let him get away with it this long. They were a relatively new team added to Blackguard Security, and the men he picked had no reason to trust him. Yet.

"My wife," he finally answered.

No one spoke, not for the solid minute it took him to get into a better position.

"Ah." Blayd was the first one to open his mouth. "Didn't realize you were married."

"I'm not," he snapped too quickly. He didn't like talking about that time in his life, and had effectively avoided it for the last ten years. No one but his boss knew the real reason he finally left the CIA after years of undercover work.

"But you just said wife," Gage reminded him.

They were the only three from his team sent on this mission. The rest of the men who made up Team Phantom were handling their own assignments. He had begged Black to send him alone. There was no reason he needed anyone else to handle one woman, but his boss refused, claiming he didn't want the hassle of cleaning up too much of a mess.

Like he would just kill Emma. No, he wanted her to suffer and a bullet to the head wouldn't accomplish that. Even if he currently had the perfect shot.

"Hard to get a divorce when the woman goes rogue and changes her name. Took me all this time to finally find her."

It was only because he went to work for David Black that he had the chance to discover where Emma was hiding this whole time. Ten long-ass years to discover that the woman he thought he would spend the rest of his life with was actually working for the enemy. The one person Daniel wanted dead more than anything. Now she was just as much his enemy.

"So, what did she do?"

He was tempted to ignore Gage's question, but he promised the man, when he brought him onto the team, that he wouldn't be like Gage's old boss. That promise was coming back to bite him in the ass early.

So instead of doing what he wanted to do, which was come up with some lie, he shut down all feelings and replied coldly. "She started working for the man who killed my daughter."

There was nothing else to say. No way for him to explain the pain he experienced all over again when Black finally got the information he longed for.

Betrayed didn't even begin to cover the emotion. At one point, Daniel had thought Emma had sacrificed for the greater good, had done what he couldn't at the time and avenged their daughter. Instead, he had found out the hard way that she was working for the same man who took their world and upended it.

Gage whistled. "I'm sorry, man."

He didn't want his new team to feel sorry for him. He didn't want anyone's apologies. They were pointless and meaningless. What he wanted was to complete the assignment and get on with his life.

Daniel knew it was rude not to answer, but he didn't give the first fuck. A person didn't earn the reputation of being ruthless because he cared what others thought of him. He made that clear when his boss approached him and asked him to put together a new team.

Daniel wasn't the leader most would want. He pulled no punches, and he refused to stroke egos. There was a good chance the men would hate him more than they liked him. He was fine with all that. He didn't want to be anyone's best friend. He just wanted to do the damn job he was hired to do.

Ridding the world of scumbags like the man who killed his daughter. That's all he cared about.

Movement inside the villa caught his attention. He let out a string of curses.

"Looks like the second target is on the move."

The primary objective, today at least, was Emma. Gutting Armando Ruis was just supposed to be a bonus, but the bonus he desperately wanted would now have to wait. A job for another day.

"Want me to follow him?" Blayd radioed through his comm.

He'd left Blayd with the SUV in case they needed to make a quick getaway, which meant it would be easy to just let him go after Armando. He was confident it wouldn't take his teammate long to catch the target, but that would mean leaving Gage without protection, and he could never be *that* much of an asshole. Too many times, the CIA left him to swing in the wind alone. He refused to do the same. He might be ruthless, but he wasn't sending anyone out on a suicide mission.

"Stand down," Daniel ordered. "We'll get another shot at him soon."

He would make sure of it. Armando would die by his hand.

Daniel continued to watch as Emma moved leisurely through the home. There was no hesitation. No stumbling. She looked completely at ease amongst the wealth, her likely designer dress fitting in with the surroundings.

This wasn't the same woman he married. The Emma he knew would never have been caught dead in a dress outside of a formal event. Even for their wedding, she threatened to elope on a beach so she could get away with shorts and a tank top.

It would seem that when she traded in her dignity, she also traded her combat boots for a pair of fancy heels. Why she needed to wear heels when casually floating around the house was beyond him, but it would make his life easier. He doubted she would be able to fight him off in that outfit.

He checked the area one more time. Confident no one would get in his way, he tapped his comm. "Let's move."

Daniel could hear Gage's breathing in his ear, but the man was nowhere in sight. Good. He didn't know a damn thing about Gage before he asked him to join the new team except that he used to work with Jaxson. Actually, he didn't know anything about any of the men he recruited, except for Liam. But each one was recommended by someone he trusted, so he would give them the benefit of the doubt.

Gage was proving to be just as good as Jaxson said he would be.

"I've got eyes on the target."

Both relief and anger flowed through him at Gage's confirmation. He'd waited years to get his revenge. Painstaking hours were spent with the dirtbags of the earth just to gain even the slightest lead. Knowing that he was just feet away from getting the answers he craved made it all worth it.

"We move on my signal," he whispered.

He counted backward in his head slowly. He couldn't fuck this up. Emma wasn't a dainty flower. She was a trained CIA operative, just like him, before she went rogue. One of the best. He couldn't let their previous connection distract him.

Once he was sure the cold, ruthless killer he had become known for was fully in place, he switched from counting down in his head to counting down for his team.

At one, he hopped up from the prone position he used to watch the villa and moved at a clipped pace until he was outside the patio door. One more deep breath and he was breaking the glass and stepping through the now shattered door.

Emma didn't scream at the sudden intrusion. She didn't seem the least bit intimidated as she glanced over her shoulder. What Daniel did see was the flicker of surprise before anger consumed her. Turning fully to face him, she charged across the room, her high heels clicking against the terracotta floor.

One solid punch connected with his jaw, but he used

her forward momentum to flip her body and send the two of them crashing to the floor. Throwing his leg over her, he straddled her hips and pinned her arms down above her head.

"Get the fuck off me."

Emma attempted to buck him off and her body tried to flail beneath him, but all she managed to do was wear herself down as he put more weight on her.

"Not a chance," he leaned down and growled in her ear. "Now it's time for you to go to sleep. We have a fucking plane to catch."

Gage swooped in and shoved the needle into her neck. Black made it very clear he was allowed to drug her, but not use physical violence to knock her out. He wasn't happy with the decision but he would get to have his fun later, after he got Emma back to New Mexico where he could interrogate her; why she chose to work for the asshole who murdered their daughter.

Then she would pay. Just like Armando would in a few days.

Daniel felt her body go limp. He waited a few extra seconds to make sure she wasn't faking it before he climbed off her and hefted her over his shoulder all in one swoop.

"On our way out. We'll meet you at the rendezvous point."

He kept his comm open until he and Gage were within a visual distance of the SUV. Daniel wasted no time tossing Emma into the back seat. Grabbing the flex cuffs, he tied her arms and legs. The drugs Gage gave her should keep her knocked out until they were well into the air, but he refused to take a chance. Nothing would fuck up this chance for him.

The drive to the small airport was quick and quiet.

Fortunately for them, Armando insisted on having his villa within a few miles of the private airstrip. It made getting in and out undetected a lot easier.

Daniel nodded to the pilot as he pulled Emma's unconscious body out of the car. Liam was technically their team pilot, but he was already out on a mission when Black confirmed Emma's location. He was given the choice to wait or use one of the other teams' pilots. Not wanting to miss the opportunity, he chose the stranger.

Phantom was the newest team and Black wanted them to be as much of a ghost as possible. So no names and no casual conversations took place as he, Gage, and Blayd walked up the stairs and took their seats inside the luxury plane. Daniel preferred it that way. He didn't join Blackguard Security because he was looking for friends. He had one mission and one mission only.

And that mission was strapped to a seat just a few feet in front of him.

"Are we headed back to New Mexico or are we going to use one of the off-site locations?"

He wished the answer to Blayd's question could be that they were headed to an off-site location. One that would be the complete opposite of the luxury Emma had been staying in, but his boss refused.

Black demanded Emma be taken to the New Mexico headquarters, the one built specifically for their team. It was secluded, built just outside the desert. They wouldn't have to worry about anyone noticing a very reluctant woman being forced against her will since it was almost a guarantee Emma would wake up before they landed. Private quarters. Private airport. It paid to be rich and Black was certainly that. He would be even more so once his team was running at full capacity because the jobs they would take, no one else would touch.

"New Mexico," he grunted, not the least bit happy that Emma would see where he lived.

"What's the plan?"

He spared no mercy as he told Gage how he planned to extract the information he needed from Emma. The mission was twofold. He wanted Emma, and their client wanted Armando, dealt with in a certain fashion.

"You always were a bit on the dramatic side."

All three men looked to find a semi-conscious Emma with a snarky smirk on her pink lips. The same lips he used to love kissing but now just repulsed him.

CHAPTER TWO

Son of a bitch!

She'd gotten soft. Become complacent.

It was the only acceptable excuse for Daniel getting the drop on her. It certainly wasn't because he was better than her, even if that's exactly what he would say. His arrogance was always going to be his downfall.

Emma didn't back down from his intense stare. Or his scowl. She knew exactly why he hated her, and she didn't care. He didn't know the whole story and she wasn't going to be the one to tell it to him. If he wanted to make assumptions, then that was on him.

"Not sure dramatic is the word most people would use to describe me."

Oh yeah. Her husband was pissed. Daniel had changed a lot in the last ten years. There wasn't even a hint of softness he showed her every time they were together. There was no love shining in his eyes, nor the laughter that got them through many sleepless nights with a newborn. He now looked at her the exact same way he looked at everyone else.

Cold.

Hard.

Ruthless.

A very small part of her wanted to miss all those things they shared, wanted to feel any emotion. Any at all. But it was too late for that. She had effectively shut off every emotion but hate a long time ago. So if Daniel thought he was going to make her feel bad about anything, he was sadly mistaken. He wasn't the only one who had changed.

"What do you want with me?"

She already knew the answer. There was only one thing a man like Daniel would want. Revenge against Armando. And her, because Daniel didn't know all of what he thought he knew.

"You don't deserve that answer yet," he snapped.

She rolled her eyes at the childish retort. He probably expected her to beg and plead to be let go, or demand answers that he refused to tell her. He would, again, be sadly mistaken. She'd spent years in hell, hardened in ways she never expected. Daniel's little tantrum was just a small blip, not worthy of her anger.

"That's fine. I'll gladly sit here and enjoy my ride to wherever you're taking me."

She closed her eyes and tried to find a more comfortable spot in the chair. It was hard considering both her wrists and ankles were bound together, but she managed.

She listened to the three men talk around her. She had no idea who the other men were, nor did she care. Daniel wasn't going to introduce them, and it didn't matter anyway. Her efforts were better spent figuring out a way to escape. She had unfinished business, and these men weren't going to slow her down.

No one spoke to her for the rest of the flight, which she

didn't mind. She used the time to regain some of the strength that whatever drug they used took away from her. She hoped to learn something from their talking, but that was wishful thinking. They didn't give her shit. Their conversations were mundane and pointless; boring to the point that she wondered if they did it purposely for her sake.

The landing was smooth, unlike the way Daniel pulled her out of her seat. If he wanted to prove just how much he hated her, he was doing a fine job of it. She didn't give him the satisfaction of complaining. She kept her mouth shut as he manhandled her off the plane and into an SUV.

Wherever they were taking her was hot. And dry. And in the middle of no-damn-where. She could see nothing but dirt. For the briefest moment, she considered that this was where her life would end. Daniel and his team were taking her to the middle of the desert to kill her and would leave her body for the crows to eat.

Emma was still formulating how she would fight back with all of her limbs tied together when the SUV rolled to a stop. Was she hallucinating, or was that a large compound in the middle of the desert? It was the only way to describe the massive one-story building sitting directly in the middle of several small buildings. All of them looked new, and all of them looked out of place, like some toddler grabbed the playhouses and dropped them into a random sandbox.

She wanted to ask where they were. She wanted to know who owned the place. Did Daniel build this place and put together this team after swearing he never wanted to work with anyone again? It had been so long. Maybe he changed his mind. She'd certainly changed over the years, so there was no reason he wouldn't have as well. That's what tragedy did to people. It changed them. Some for the better and, like in her case, some for the worst.

In the end, it was her pride that won out, and the reason she didn't ask the burning questions. She let whichever goon of Daniel's carry her over his shoulder and into an interrogation room. She supposed she should be happy it wasn't a dungeon or basement. There were no tools around that implied they planned to torture her. Not in this room, at least. She would consider herself lucky for the time being. She was strapped to the one lone chair in the room and left by herself.

Emma knew what Daniel was doing. She herself had done it a million times while working with the CIA. He was hoping to make her sweat. To give her time alone to agonize over what he planned to do with her. It was likely he thought she had gone soft since the last time he saw her. The heels and dress she wore did an excellent job of tricking people into thinking she wasn't a threat. Daniel was wrong. She was just as much a threat now as she had been when they were married.

Well, they were still married. Or at least she thought so. There were probably laws out there about abandoning a spouse for ten years that allowed Daniel to be free of her, but they never signed papers. They never spoke about divorce. They were together one day, and she was gone the next, handling things as she saw fit despite the objections she knew her husband would make.

The door opened once again, but instead of Daniel, one of the other men from the plane entered and leaned against the wall right in front of her. His massive arms were crossed over his chest and a scowl was on his face.

He didn't speak. Just pierced her with his constant stare.

"As much as I welcome a good staring contest, you know the kind where you look into someone's soul and realize they're the one?" She smirked. "You're just not my type. I'm sorry."

She gave him her most dazzling smile. She refused to be intimidated by a man she didn't know. If Daniel thought this would soften her up, then he was dead wrong. Daniel was better off coming in to speak with her himself. If he wanted a confrontation, then the only person she would give it to was her husband.

The stranger merely lifted his one shoulder. "No hard feelings. I don't do married women anyway. Just not my style."

The harsh comeback was given with its own smile. Except she had to give the guy credit, his was much better because it included the sexiest dimple on the left side that she ever saw.

Well, fuck!

Well played, Daniel. She had a thing for nice smiles and this guy's was the nicest she'd seen in a long time, but she wouldn't let it sway her. She was tougher than that.

"Since it would appear Daniel is too much of a coward to come face me himself, how about you tell me your name."

"Blayd."

Huh. Well, that didn't go as she planned. She fully expected him to tell her to go to hell. Shaking herself out of the surprised stupor, she smiled once again.

"Well, it's nice to meet you, Blayd." *Weird name.* "I'm Emma, but I'm going to assume you already know that, considering you're friends with my ex. Now that we know each other, how about you be a gentleman and untie me."

"Husband, not ex."

She reared back as if he had slapped her. "Excuse me?"

"You said I was friends with your ex," he answered matter-of-factly. "The way I hear it, the two of you never divorced, so technically he's still your husband."

Blayd's casual-as-fuck attitude was starting to grate on her nerves. Smile or not, whoever this guy was, she preferred her damn *husband*. At least she knew what to expect from him.

"Semantics," she huffed. "How about you just go get Daniel and let's get this show on the road? I'm sure everyone is busy and I know damn well I have better things I could be doing rather than sitting here entertaining you."

Again, Blayd surprised her when he simply tipped his head back and laughed. "I get what Daniel saw in you. You got spunk. If you weren't already taken, I would gladly take you for a roll in the sheets. I bet you're just as feisty there as well."

With that parting shot, Blayd walked back out of the room.

She was stunned silent. She never thought it would be possible, but there was always a first. She would give this round to Blayd. Whatever Daniel's game plan was, it was working. She would need to regroup and build back up her defenses before the next round.

CHAPTER THREE

"I know you aren't happy with me, but I have my reasons."

Daniel didn't bother to look over at his new boss and Black didn't expect a confirmation. His boss knew what he was getting long before he was hired. Daniel didn't play well with others. He made no secret of it. And he certainly didn't plan to change.

He was surprised his boss even showed up. This wasn't headquarters. That was located up north, in Maine. When Black asked him about creating a new team, it was the only stipulation Daniel provided—he needed to be close to Texas. Close to Jaxson who was living there with his wife, who also happened to be a member of his team. Jaxson was the only member who wouldn't live in New Mexico with the rest of them.

"You don't need to be here. I have the situation under control."

Daniel watched the CCTV screen as Blayd entered the holding room. He could almost predict what Emma was going to say before it came out of her mouth. He hated how well he still knew the woman.

"I know you have it under control, but there's a lot riding on this, so I thought it best I checked in. I knew you wouldn't be eager to report in, nor would you come up to Maine if I asked."

No, he wouldn't go back to that godforsaken state. Never again. It held too many memories. Just like the woman in the other room. Killing her on the spot would've prevented those memories, but that option was taken from him.

"You seem awfully invested in my ex," Daniel growled.

He had ignored all the warning bells when Black first gave him the information needed to find Emma because he wanted his revenge so badly. Now it made him wonder what Black's true intentions were. Something was off, but he didn't know what.

"We were all friends at one point, or did you forget that?"

No, he couldn't forget the connection they all had.

"Besides, you've waited ten years for this and now you have a problem because I'm not letting you kill her in cold blood? Because I'm saving your morality by not letting you commit murder?"

Screw his morality. That died the longer he was forced to live without his daughter in his life. Getting revenge for her meant more to him than anything else. He would gladly go to jail if it meant Emma paid for her crimes.

The question didn't deserve an answer, so he didn't bother to justify how he felt. Daniel continued to listen to Emma and nearly punched the wall when Blayd implied he'd like to fuck her. Daniel didn't want to feel a damn thing toward her. She was the enemy, not his wife. What she did in private didn't matter. She was nothing to him.

Liar!

He hated that she was still beautiful. It annoyed him that such a pretty face could hide such an ugly core. He had hoped that her darker blonde locks had faded into a scraggly gray. Instead, they looked just as soft as when he used to run his fingers through them each night. Nothing about her outer appearance had changed to reflect the evil person she had become.

"Blayd sure knows how to get under her skin. I didn't think it was possible to render Emma speechless."

Daniel relaxed his fist for the third time in under a minute. He needed to get himself under control before Blayd walked back into the surveillance room.

"She's not going to break easily," Blayd laughed as he joined them. "She seems like the type who goes straight for the jugular."

"That she does," Daniel snapped. "So it would be best if you didn't entertain thoughts of fucking her."

Blayd didn't seem the least bit worried by the threat. The man had the nerve to actually smirk at him.

"Don't worry. She's not my type, despite what I said. I'm not into cougars."

A low rumble moved through his throat. He wasn't that damn old. He and Liam were only a solid ten years older than the rest of the guys on his team. Not that Blayd was that young; he was closer to forty than he was thirty but that was still a lot younger than Daniel's nearly fifty years. Emma was the same age. Never did he think age would matter to him when he operated because he still felt young, but Blayd's comment hit a mark he hadn't known existed.

"It's obvious she wants you in there."

No shit, Captain Fucking Obvious! This was why he liked to work alone. There was no chance of people giving him stupid observations that he didn't need.

"She's not the one in charge."

Daniel stormed out of the room. He needed to move, to work off some of the pent-up frustration pumping through his body. Watching Emma through the camera wasn't working anymore. If he didn't put space between them, he would act without thinking and then he would be forced to deal with a pissed-off Black.

"You need to rein yourself in before you go in to question her about Armando."

Daniel respected his boss. He was one of the only people he still spoke to from those days before everything went to shit. But right now, friend or not, Black was ticking him off.

"I know we were all friends once, but don't tell me how to handle my wife," he snapped. "Not after what she did."

He needed to stop thinking of her as his wife. She was nothing to him anymore. Maybe if he repeated that a few hundred more times, it would finally sink in.

"I told you when you took this job that there was a lot for you to learn. Not all things are what they appear."

"I know damn well what you said."

"Stubborn asshole." Black shook his head. "Too damn stubborn for your own good."

The frustration he was hoping to work out was tighter than it had been before he left the observation room. Any discussion that involved Emma seemed to do that to him. He thought he was over it. Thought he could finally handle things with a cold detachment, but every second Emma was back in his life was proving him wrong.

He was about to give Black a *fuck off* response when he noticed Gage moving at a fast clip down the hallway toward him.

"We have a problem."

His guard immediately went up. He was ready to spin on his heel and go make sure that Emma was still in the building, but Black stopped him with a hand to the chest.

"What kind of problem?" Black asked.

Gage turned to their boss. "The villa we took Emma from just blew up. There's nothing left of the place but ash."

Daniel pushed Black's hand away and moved into Gage's space. "Was Armando in the villa when it blew up?"

Gage shook his head. "We have no way of knowing. We only got notification because a local was keeping an eye on the area for anything strange. He reached out when the place blew up, but he has no idea if Armando was there or not. No one saw him after he left earlier today, before we grabbed Emma. I would go with the assumption that Armando is still on the loose."

Shit. Now Armando would be in the wind and it would take them longer to find him and drag out the fucking assignment. He just wanted this dealt with already.

Only one person could give him the information he needed and he was done screwing around.

Turning, Daniel stomped his way to the interrogation room. He didn't stop until her neck was beneath his palm and he was pushing her back, consuming her space.

"Tell me where the fuck I can find Armando," he growled. "And while you're at it, explain who else wanted you or the fucker dead."

CHAPTER FOUR

She should probably be scared. The look in Daniel's eyes screamed that he would end her life and not feel an ounce of remorse. Emma knew he hated her, and was well aware that would happen when she decided on the path she would take, but she hadn't cared. The loss of a child broke her in ways that could never be healed. She was prepared to die for the cause she took up. It appeared that time was closer than she realized.

"You know exactly where to find him," she ground out despite the pressure on her throat. "The same place you took me from."

Her answer only seemed to piss him off more, and the hand wrapped around her neck squeezed ever so slightly. Her breathing was coming shallower. But still, she refused to show any fear.

"And that villa was blown up after we left and not by us. Which tells me someone hates one of you more than I do. An accomplishment really."

Fuck. All of the information she'd gathered over the years was gone. Just like that. Destroyed. Years spent sacrificing her soul. All for nothing. She would never learn the truth now.

"Was Armando in there?"

She didn't think it was possible for Daniel's dark eyes to get any darker, but right now they were practically black. There was no distinction between the iris and pupil anymore. She had never seen him so angry, and for the first time since he captured her, fear reared its ugly head. She didn't want to die. Not until she completed her mission, and not at the hands of her husband. She had thought she was prepared, but it was all a lie. He couldn't kill her until after.

"Afraid your boyfriend is dead?" He squeezed a little tighter. "That all those expensive luxuries you got accustomed to will no longer be available?" Even tighter. "Don't worry, Em. He's still alive for another day, but it won't be for much longer. I'll be sure of that."

She knew what Daniel thought of her. She knew what story he believed because it was the one she set up when she asked for a new identity, but it still hurt that he could so easily think the worst of her. Nothing. Their years together meant nothing to him it would seem. Well, screw him. That fear she thought she felt was now just anger.

"Go. To. Hell."

The last word was more of a croak. Daniel was going to slowly kill her. The more hatred that poured out of him, the tighter he squeezed. Black dots were floating in her vision, blocking out his sexy face. A horrible thought to have at the moment. She wasn't supposed to find him sexy anymore. But her mind had other plans. If this was going to be the way she died, at least it was looking at the only man she loved. Her only regret was that he didn't know all the facts before he executed her. He was going to kill her believing a lie, and when he discovered the truth, it would destroy him.

"Let her go, man. You can't murder her."

Whoever was speaking sounded far away. At the end of a tunnel. She could swear people were arguing but the voices no longer made sense. She couldn't get enough air. Her body was shutting down, sending all of the remaining oxygen to her vital organs before nothing was left. The blackness was sucking her down. Begging for her to join it.

Just when she thought it was all over, and her final thought would be that she could finally join her daughter, the pressure on her throat lifted and she was crashing to the floor. She barely registered the pain in her shoulder as it met the cold hard tile.

Her starved lungs begged for oxygen and her brain tried to make sense of what was happening. The yelling around her continued.

"Emma, are you alright?"

It was several moments before she could answer Black and the most she could manage was a simple nod.

"Are you fucking *insane*?" She barely recognized that voice, but she thought it was from the plane ride. "I understand you hate her, but she's still cuffed, asshole."

"Shallow breaths, Emma. Just take it slow."

Black's face filled her vision. The dots from just moments ago slowly started to recede. But now she was more confused than anything. Why was he here?

"I'm ... okay." She tried to keep her voice from shaking, but knew she missed the mark when Black's face went from concerned to pissed off.

"Don't bullshit me, Emma. Daniel nearly strangled you to death. That's not okay."

He was right. She never thought he would go that far. He wasn't a murderer. At least, not the man she used to know. But grief changed people, and in Daniel's case, she feared it was for the worst.

"You're right." She tried to swallow around the pain in her throat. "But I'm fine. I swear."

"Get him the fuck out of here!" Black turned and snapped at someone outside of her periphery. "It's confession time, Emma. I refuse to watch you die on this damn mountain you seem so sure to stand on."

She tried to struggle against Black's hold. "No, it's too early. I can still finish what I started."

He couldn't pull her away. Not when she was so close. Not after all the time she spent. He knew all the hard work she put in. He knew ...

"Why are you here, Black? How did you know Daniel took me?"

The loss of oxygen to her brain was making her slow. Black's sudden presence should've set warning bells off way before this. It made no sense that he was here. Wherever here was.

He didn't look the least bit remorseful as he told her, "Because I sent him."

SHE WAS MOVED to a different room. This one looked to be more of an office, and she was no longer cuffed. She sat on one of the only two pieces of furniture in the room—a leather couch that was tucked against one wall. A desk was directly across from her. Nothing else. Not a single picture, chair, or hell, even a random pen was tossed around. She doubted anyone used the office. Or maybe someone hadn't moved into it yet because it still smelled of fresh paint.

After Black dropped the bomb that he was the one to

send Daniel to get her, he dumped her inside the office and left. He said he needed time to calm her husband down before he felt comfortable putting them in the same room again.

Daniel wasn't the only one who needed protection from her. Give her two minutes alone with her boss and she would show him exactly how she felt about him pulling her out of her assignment. Armando was hers. She gave up everything to be the one to end his miserable life. Spent years earning his trust, and for what?

Nothing.

She grew more pissed off with each passing minute, so by the time Black graced her with his presence, she forgot all about the fact that just an hour earlier, Daniel had tried to kill her. She was ready for a fight and Black was just the man she wanted to fight with.

"Sit down before you fall down."

Black pointed to her as she launched herself off the couch. Her boss wasn't the least bit phased by the anger pouring off her.

"I'm not that weak. He tried to strangle me, not chop off my legs. Once I got oxygen back to my brain, I was fine. You had no right to break my cover."

Black got right up in her face. Fire practically shot from his eyes as he towered over her.

"I'm your *boss*, or did you forget that? You knew damn well when you signed on with me that there would come a time when you could be pulled off this assignment. That was at my discretion, and I'm calling it."

The two of them were in such a heated discussion that they hadn't heard anyone else approach until Daniel's voice broke through.

"What do you mean, you're her boss?"

CHAPTER FIVE

There's no way he could've heard Black correctly. Emma and his boss turned in his direction, but neither bothered to answer him.

"I asked you a fucking question, Black. What do you mean, you're her boss?"

Black had the nerve to look between him and Emma. His wife tried to shake her head no, but his boss didn't seem to care that she was objecting.

"When Emma went rogue, she came to me. Asked for help infiltrating Armando's ranks."

He didn't stop and think. Daniel turned and put his fist into his office wall. The office he loathed because it reminded him of all the things he never wanted to be: in charge of others.

Black didn't stop speaking despite his outburst.

"I gave her a new cover. Set her up, and for the last nearly ten years, Emma has slowly worked her way up until she was able to gain Armando's trust."

Daniel couldn't turn around. He couldn't look at his boss or his wife, not when he knew what he would see. The angry red marks on Emma's neck were prominent. It was the first thing he noticed when he stepped through the doorway. Seconds ago he had been proud, knowing that he was one step closer to getting revenge for his daughter. Now he was confused and angry for a different reason.

With both fists firmly planted against the wall and his head hanging down, he asked between clenched teeth, "You knew her whereabouts all along?"

"Yes, I did."

There wasn't a hint of remorse. And later, when he had a chance to think about it, he would probably realize that was the reason for his next action. Pushing off the wall, Daniel spun and let his fist connect with Black's jaw.

"Daniel," Emma gasped, but he ignored her.

"You"—another punch—"knew this"—one more punch—"whole time?"

His fist was cocked back to throw another punch, but before he could make the connection, a hard body slammed into him.

"Have you lost your mind." Gage slammed him into the floor again when he tried to fight off the hold. "You attacked our boss!"

He and Gage continued to fight for control. Daniel was pissed off enough to be a good match for Gage's brute strength. The man was a tank; he had an easy six inches on him and almost seventy-five pounds of muscle. On any other day, he wouldn't even consider going hand to hand with his teammate, but he wasn't thinking clearly anymore.

He was breaking his one rule: do not allow anger to influence his decisions. He was doing that a lot today, a lot of irrational choices that he would regret later.

"Settle the fuck down before you hurt yourself."

With one last body slam from Gage, all of the fight left

him, and Daniel dropped his head onto the floor behind him with a thud. His arms flopped down next to him. They were both breathing heavily and Gage still straddled him. Shame washed over him. He focused solely on his teammate, ignoring the rest of the people in the room.

"You can let me up. I won't hit anyone else."

Gage hesitated. Daniel didn't blame him. He made sure his eyes showed his sincerity. All of the anger he felt for the last ten years suddenly drained out of him. When Gage finally let him, Daniel took his time to sit up, but he kept his head down. He wasn't ready to confront the damage he had done. Humiliation, a feeling he wasn't used to, consumed him.

"Why didn't you tell me?"

He didn't know if he was asking Black or Emma. Or maybe it was just a question for himself. Everything he thought he knew was suddenly turned upside down, and he didn't know how to handle it.

For years, he thought the worst of his wife. Thought she betrayed him when she left without a trace. That betrayal was the reasoning for every decision he made, every assignment he took. It only got worse when he learned *why* she was gone. And Black knew all of that. The whole time, his boss knew the truth and kept it from him. The entire situation was fucked, and he didn't know what to do.

"I asked him not to."

It took herculean efforts, but he looked up and met Emma's hard expression. The red marks on her neck were just another reminder of the mistakes he made and the anger he let take over. When he first placed his hands around her neck, it was just to scare her. He never meant for it to go that far. The blinding rage consumed him and now he would need to live with that.

"Why?"

There was no more heat when he spoke. He was genuinely curious. Why would she spend all this time lying to him? And why did Black help her?

"Because you weren't in the right headspace after Kali died. You would've tried to stop me. You threw yourself into work, you felt that doing your job was the best way to get justice for our daughter. You wanted the system to work. I didn't. I knew better, so I made the decision to do whatever was necessary to get results. Black understood that as well. I begged him to help me and I warned him not to tell you. I would rather you think the worst of me than try to stop me"

"Mission accomplished."

Daniel pushed himself up off the floor. He took a moment to look at Black. Blood dripped from a cut on his eye and from a broken nose. He would need to apologize for that later. Right now, he needed to go for a walk, to think about everything Emma told him. It was a lot to process.

He thought back to when Kali was killed. They had been on vacation, visiting an island and out for dinner. Their daughter had begged them to go for a walk afterwards. She'd wanted to see all the pretty lights. Daniel had known it might not be safe. There were rumors about tourists getting hurt. Islanders advised staying on the resort grounds, but when Kali asked, how could he say no? His daughter died because he couldn't tell her no.

It had been Emma who learned Armando's name. Daniel had taken time off from work those weeks after Kali died, but Emma went right back. She used every contact the agency had to find out a name. He had used that as an argument for why they should continue to let the agency handle the investigation. Emma disagreed. It was the last fight they had before she disappeared. He was ashamed to admit he was a coward at the time.

It would be years of no progress before he started to agree that maybe Emma was right, but by that time, Emma was gone. He couldn't find a trace of her, didn't have a clue where she was or if she was even alive. Not until Black found her and informed him she had changed her name.

"Don't blame Black."

Daniel had been so distracted wandering through the building that he hadn't realized Emma had followed him.

"Go away, Emma. I need some time."

He needed a lot of time and he was pretty sure that even then, he still wouldn't be able to wrap his head around everything going on. He should be used to betrayal by now, but he never thought it would come from his best friend.

"And I'll give you that time just as soon as you listen to me. This is on me. I made the decision to work for Armando. Yes, Black helped me, but only because he knew, either way, I was going. He made it as safe for me as he could. I didn't want you to know what I was doing. He was never supposed to tell you. I was this close," she hissed. "*This close* to ending Armando and then he brought you in. So you don't get to be pissed at Black because in the end, he chose you anyway."

Daniel listened to her retreating footsteps.

Yeah, maybe Black chose him in the end, but he chose to help Emma first.

DANIEL WAS BREATHING HEAVILY AGAIN, but this time for a completely different reason. Ten miles on the treadmill and he still hadn't worked through the emotions coursing through his body. He went back and forth between being angry at Emma and Black, and understanding why they did what they did.

It's true, he wasn't in the right head space after Kali's death. Nothing Emma said would've mattered, so he understood why she made the decision. It was the years after that bothered him. He'd kept in contact with Black his whole life. His friend knew about his struggles with the CIA, knew about the assignments he went on. How for years he was an undercover hitman and how that was the tipping point that led to him leaving the CIA. Black was his only confidant and friend. And still, the man lied to him.

"Figured I would find you here. Running was always your outlet."

He stopped the treadmill and stepped onto the sides. He gave himself time to get his heart rate back to a reasonable beat before he turned and met his boss's gaze.

"What do you want, Black?"

Someone had reset his boss's nose and placed a butterfly stitch over the cut. Black had changed out of his bloody shirt, so he was back to looking like the clean-cut billionaire he was. No one would know that under all that polish was a murderer, just like the rest of the men on his team.

"I understand why you're pissed, and if the situation were reversed, then I would be too, but I had good reasons."

All the running he had just done to work through the pent-up frustration was for nothing.

"There are no good reasons for lying to me. I told you three years ago that I was ready to find Emma. You could've told me at any point since then, but you didn't. You let me believe that you suddenly found her and that she was working for Armando," he snapped.

"That was the agreement I had with Emma. I broke that

agreement when I felt it was important."

He couldn't stand still any longer. The calm and emotionless demeanor that people associated him with was nowhere to be found.

"You lied to me! You hired me under false pretenses. How the fuck am I supposed to believe anything you tell me from here on out? You know damn well that honesty is important to me. Why should I bother staying?"

Daniel left the CIA because of lies. He had a pretty decent setup working for Wes, but avenging his daughter meant he could never truly feel settled. That was the only reason he let Black convince him to lead this new team. A responsibility he hadn't wanted but would take because it meant finally following through on the only thing that got him through life these past years.

"Yes, I did, and I'm not sorry. I needed Emma out and you were the perfect excuse."

Daniel turned to his boss, ready to hit the man all over again.

"But," Black continued, "only because I knew you needed this. You might not realize it now, but this team is exactly what you need in your life. A fresh start. Just give it a chance."

Fuck Black for thinking he knew what was best for him. Friend or not, he had no right. Now this new venture that he was so sure would be a great new start for him was tainted.

"You had no right manipulating me."

"Maybe not, but I did it. Now you need to decide how you plan on living with it now that you know the truth."

Daniel watched Black walk away. He had a choice to make, and he didn't have the first clue what direction to turn.

CHAPTER SIX

Emma's throat still hurt. She didn't bother to look in the mirror because she already knew what she would see. Red handprint marks that would turn to bruising sooner rather than later. Daniel had almost killed her. Her own husband, the man she pledged her life to, hated her more than she realized. It shouldn't surprise her, and yet it did. But she had other things to worry about.

"What do we know about the villa?"

She was still in the office, but now the only one with her was the same man who tackled Daniel.

"Nothing except it was flattened and our contact in the area states Armando never returned after we picked you up."

Son of a bitch! All of the information she had collected was in that house. Armando was security conscious and had more firewalls than anyone else she'd ever met. It made digital copies nearly impossible, so she went old school; she made physical copies and hid them in a loose floorboard in her bedroom. If the house was leveled, then everything she had was gone. She needed that information.

One quick rap on the door nearly had her jumping out of her skin. This wasn't who she was. She didn't scare easily. She was still mentally chastising herself when Daniel walked in.

"Gage, can I have a moment to speak with Emma?"

Gage looked genuinely torn at the request. She didn't know the man, but felt she owed him reassurance. "It's okay."

"I'm not going to lay a hand on her."

Whether it was her reassurance or Daniel's proclamation, Gage finally slipped out of the room.

With her arms crossed over her chest, Emma met Daniel head-on. "Glad to hear I don't have a strangling in my future. I know I like things a little rough, but even that was a little too far for me."

Daniel dropped his eyes to the floor.

"Too soon," she laughed. It was either that or cry, and she wasn't going to do that. She had been through tougher times. "Lighten up, Daniel. I've dealt with worse in my lifetime."

That did the trick. The defeat she witnessed when he walked in was erased. She much preferred the cold, calculated man to the one who stood before her moments ago. This man she knew how to handle.

"That's not funny, Emma. I lost control, and for that, I am truly sorry."

She was shocked into silence. Her husband never apologized. Not sincerely, anyway. It was always laced with sarcasm. He didn't do it when they worked together and never when they were married. It was one of the things she both loved and hated about him. He didn't sugarcoat things, and he didn't offer her words just to placate her. Things were real, and she missed that over the years.

"Fine." She dropped her arms down to her sides. "Apology accepted. Although I'm shocked as hell you even offered one. That's not like you. But now can we change the subject? Armando is still out there and you screwed up all the progress I made."

Daniel was assessing her for sincerity. It didn't take knowing him for years to see what he was doing. Despite the cold-hearted man he tried to be, Daniel had a soft spot. He would hate it if she ever called him on it, would deny it until his dying breath, but she knew. She always knew. It was what made him a great father. It was why he took Kali's death harder and needed more time to come to the realization of what really needed to happen to avenge her.

"What did you do for Armando?"

It was her turn to look away. Spinning on her heels, she paced the small office and took a few seconds to gather her thoughts. For too long, she had to be someone else, to live as someone else. There was a time she wondered if she would ever be able to go back to the woman she used to be.

"I did whatever it took to earn his trust. I handled his bookings. I funneled his money. I purchased him"—she took a big gulp—"women. I did every despicable thing he asked of me so that I could figure out who hired him."

"What?"

This was the part she was hoping she would never have to tell Daniel. She wanted to come back to him when everything was finished and let him know she handled things without him knowing the truth. Now it was too late. She was tired of the lies. Tired of hiding everything. Maybe Black was right to pull her when he did.

"Armando was just the hired gun. Someone else is responsible for Kali's death. I was gaining Armando's trust so that I could find out who that was. I was close before you took me."

If there was furniture in the room aside from the desk, she was sure Daniel would've destroyed it. He looked like a caged animal, prepared to rip anything and everything up. This angry side of him was so new that she didn't know how to help him control it.

"Did Black know?" Daniel seethed.

"Yes, I knew someone else was responsible for Kali's death, and yes, I knew she was close to finding out who."

Her boss had really shitty timing. This was becoming a trend and she would need to reconsider working for him, if that was the case.

"So why the hell did you send my team in after her?" Daniel demanded.

"Because she was compromised," Black snapped. She'd never heard him use that tone with anyone before. But it was the words that shocked her the most.

"No," she denied. "There's no way."

She had been so careful, had taken every measure to ensure Armando had no idea what she was doing. There was no way Armando could've known. He would've killed her as soon as he found out. Armando showed no mercy. If he felt she betrayed him, then she would be dead. She was positive about that.

"Yes. I was notified that a hit was put out for you. I knew I needed to act, so I gave Daniel the information he had been seeking for years and let him put a team together. I knew he would act quickly. Fortunately for you, his team is nothing like the others I employ."

"What exactly does that mean? And don't give me the political answer."

She was so tired of Black and his riddles. She just

wanted someone to give her a straight answer for once. The cloak-and-dagger bullshit was getting old. She lived it, but if he was going to insist she be brought back to the real world, then he was going to start telling her the truth. She deserved as much.

"Plain and simple, Daniel's team is nothing but mercenaries. They took the hit that was put out on you and Armando. 'Two birds, one stone' kind of thing."

She couldn't believe what she was hearing. Blackguard Security was a legitimate business. It was why she went to him when she needed help. She knew he would keep her walking as close to the right side of the law as possible.

Nothing about what Black was telling her sounded that way.

"So, you just kill innocent people?"

She looked around for Daniel. She wasn't sure what she was hoping to gain from it, but she didn't get what she needed. His expression was purposely blank.

"No, the jobs Daniel takes are not innocent," Black answered from him. "They're criminals like Armando. Bigger fish want them dead and we make it happen. Then we keep the information on who hired his team for future reference. It's a win-win."

It sounded like a suicide mission to her. Backstabbing criminals wasn't exactly a solid business plan.

"You're gambling with their lives."

"We knew exactly what we were getting into when we took the job." Daniel's voice was flat. "Black was transparent with us from the beginning."

"And you're just okay with it?" Because she wasn't. Having her husband put his life on the line bothered her more than she cared to admit.

Emma was ready to pull her hair out. Nothing about

this day was going as she planned. There were too many things for her to wrap her mind around.

"Yes, I am. I've done a lot of awful things since the last time we saw each other. At least now I'm in control of the assignments I take." Daniel looked at David. "At least for the most part."

She stormed over to where Daniel stood. "This isn't you. This isn't the man I married. The one who so lovingly held our daughter."

Emma went toe-to-toe with him, but he didn't back down.

"You're right. I'm no longer that man. Kali's death changed me. It might've taken me longer than it did you, but I changed. I stayed with the CIA for years, and that changed me even more. It turned me into the man I am today and that might not be someone you like, but that's too damn bad. I did what I needed to survive and I don't regret it."

It made no sense. She was blaming him for essentially doing the exact same thing she did. The difference was she had hoped to return one day to the man who stood by her and now that man no longer existed. Everything that got her through the last ten years was gone. Poof. No longer available.

"Just like that?"

"Yes, just like that."

For the first time since waking up on the plane, Emma took the time to really look at Daniel. He had definitely changed since she last saw him. His dark hair had just a hint of gray peppered throughout. There were more stress lines on his forehead and around his eyes. His mouth held a perpetual frown rather than the smile he would give their daughter. But none of that took away from his appeal.

He wasn't as tall as Gage or Black. At just shy of six feet, Daniel was considered shorter, but what he lacked in height, he made up for in width. Her husband always reminded her of a linebacker with his wide shoulders and tree trunks for thighs. Physically, he looked exactly like what he said he became.

Cold.

Hard.

Ruthless.

"Fine, do whatever you like." She brushed Daniel off and turned to Black. "Can I leave now? It's been a long day, and I'd really like to rest."

"Yes, but you will be staying here at the compound with one of the team. I don't trust you not to leave the first chance you get."

She tried to scoff at her boss like she was offended, but her whole heart wasn't into it. He was right. The first chance she got, she would leave and go after Armando. She spent too many years to just give up now.

"Do I get a say in who I stay with?"

Her choices sucked. She couldn't stay with Daniel for obvious reasons. Blayd hit on her, and even though she knew he didn't mean it, she felt that would be awkward. That left Gage. He seemed protective of her in a way that didn't creep her out. But before she could give her opinion, the decision was made for her.

"No, you'll be staying with me."

CHAPTER SEVEN

Daniel opened his mouth before he could fully think the repercussions through and now he was stuck living in the same house as his wife. Black was all too happy to agree before he could take it back.

"My house is this way."

He didn't stop to make sure Emma was following him. Black felt she needed a babysitter, but it wouldn't be him. He would provide her with a place to sleep, but that was it.

"For someone who made this suggestion, you seem extremely pissed off about it." Emma smirked.

"I *am* pissed off about it," he grumbled. "I opened my mouth without thinking."

And he was doing it again. He was giving Emma the ammunition she needed by speaking what was on his mind. If he were smart, he would keep his mouth shut while she was here.

"There's the honesty I prefer. I almost forgot how good it felt to be around someone who spoke the truth for once."

Daniel left the main building and crossed the long dirt path to the first house in the cul-de-sac. When Black designed the place, he had asked each team member if they wanted to live together inside the main building where individual rooms were located opposite of the offices, or have their own houses. Some chose a house, like himself, while others opted for rooms. Now he wished he had chosen one of the rooms. Maybe then his stupid mouth wouldn't have gotten him into the position he was in. Black could've locked her in one of the damn rooms and put a guard on her.

"Do you plan on giving me the silent treatment the entire time I'm here? If so, we're going to be really bored."

He spun around so fast that Emma was forced to come to a screeching halt or risk crashing into him.

A deep rumble moved through his chest. "There are plenty of ways we could keep ourselves occupied, if that's what you're worried about."

Daniel let his eyes roam over her body. Her dress was ripped and dirty from being taken hostage by his team. Her hair had the just-fucked look despite not actually being fucked, but it was the handprints on her neck that ruined the illusion.

He took one giant step back, giving his dick the chance to settle down after being too close to her. He needed to put some distance between them. He already proved today that he didn't have his shit on lockdown.

"Oh no, don't do that." Now it was Emma crowding his space. "Don't look me over like you want to fuck me where we stand and then suddenly see my neck and pity me. I'm not some damsel who needs saving. You fucked up, you apologized, and now it's over. I'm not holding a grudge because if the situation were reversed and I had the information you were given, then I would've done the same damn thing."

"Really? You would've strangled me?" he challenged. "Choked the life out of me in front of other people?"

Emma's strength was one of the many things he loved about her. She didn't need him to save her. She didn't need to lean on him. Challenging her was foreplay and he almost forgot about that until now.

She stuck her finger into his chest repeatedly as she spoke, driving her answer home. "No, I would've shot you in the leg and interrogated you until you told me the truth. If I learned you really betrayed me, then I would've killed you without hesitation."

Her words turned him on more than any sexy lingerie ever could. Wrapping his hand around the back of her neck, he hauled her up and crashed his lips to hers. He didn't kiss her gently. He didn't coax her to open up for him. He demanded it with brutal force. He relished when she met his kiss with the same fervor. Tongues dueled. Teeth clashed. The pain she inflicted on his back with her nails spurred him on.

Trailing his one hand down her spine, he wrapped the other one around her back and let it drift lower until he cupped her ass, lifting her until her tight dress ripped just a little more as he wrapped her legs around his waist.

"I'm going to fuck you until you forget that pity you thought you saw on my face." A low rumble moved through his chest. He spun them around and slammed her body against the brick siding.

"Good." She bit his shoulder and had him so hard that he was willing to fuck her out in the open. "I only want to feel you for the rest of the night."

He fumbled with the key and cursed when he was forced to take his attention away from her and concentrate on opening the door.

"Did you really just snarl at the key?"

Yes. Yes, he did.

"With all the fucking technology Black insists on having, there should be something better than having to dig for a fucking key when one's hands are occupied."

Emma buried her face in his neck and laughed. He missed that sound.

"I'm pretty sure this wasn't what he was thinking about when he designed the system."

No, Black wouldn't be thinking that he would be struggling to unlock his door while his wife's body was wrapped around him. If someone would've told him this would be a problem an hour ago, he would've knocked them out.

The door finally gave way and Daniel stepped into the dark. He didn't bother turning on a light. There wasn't any furniture to stumble over. He slammed the door shut and tossed the keys on the floor. He could find them later.

Now that the obstacle was out of his way, he went back to feasting on his wife. He kissed her neck and nibbled on her jaw. He slipped his fingers under the edge of her panties and massaged the globes of her ass.

"Fuck, you taste good. Like temptation and sugar, all wrapped in one."

He dropped her onto his bed and watched as the moonlight bathed over her, as he pulled his shirt over his head and tossed it to the floor. He continued to watch her as he pulled the zipper down on his pants and pushed them, and his boxers, off his legs. He didn't take his eyes off her when he stepped out of them and kicked them across the room.

"I hope you're not a fan of this dress."

He didn't let her answer. He grabbed the part that was already ripped and tugged. Tearing the dress in half and exposing her almost naked body. There was nothing fancy about the simple cotton panties and bra. His wife might've been forced to wear things she hated on the outside, but she was true to herself underneath.

"I fucking hated it."

That had his lips slightly turning up. There was the wife he knew and loved. With a gentleness she wouldn't see again for a while, he slipped her panties down her legs and peeled them off. The heels were going to stay for now. He was going to enjoy feeling them dig into his back as he slammed into her.

He settled himself between her legs, and using his wide shoulders, he pushed her legs farther apart until his face was lined up with her core.

"I missed this pretty pussy. I'm going to enjoy feasting on it until you scream."

He looked up just in time to see her catch the left inside edge of her lower lip between her teeth. It was the sexiest fucking thing and had him almost coming right then. He rolled his hips slightly to ease the ache. He would be inside her soon enough, but first ...

With a flattened tongue, he licked the seam of her drenched lips. One taste and he was a goner, jolted straight into the past and all the amazing times they shared. He nibbled and sucked, and when Emma's hands clamped down onto his hair so she could force him to do what she wanted, he slipped two fingers into her tight sheath and curled them up. He found the spot that he knew from experience made her wild.

Emma pulled the hair from his roots. She ground her pussy against him and rode his face with abandon. He knew he had her when his teeth grazed her nub. He lapped up her juices and felt her body nearly melt into the mattress.

"Holy fuck, I forgot how good you were at that."

He didn't hide his smile as he crawled up her body. With one arm wrapped around her back, he hauled her farther up the bed until her blonde hair fanned his pillow.

"I'm only just getting started."

He captured her lips, letting her taste herself, letting her know just how intoxicating she was. He teased her entrance but should've known she wouldn't let him get away with that. Not giving a damn about the pace he set, she dug her nails and heels into his ass and pulled him forward until he was seated completely inside her.

"Patience was never your virtue." He bit the corner of her mouth.

"I've waited ten years to fuck you again. I call that a shit ton of patience." Her heels dug in more and he stopped thinking and just let his body feel.

He let Emma take control, met each punishing thrust with his own, let years of celibacy and pent-up sexual frustration loose. He touched. He tasted. He re-explored her and all the subtle changes that came with age. Daniel reacquainted himself with the body that was made for him—the hard lines and soft skin.

"You ... should ... never ... have ... left." Each word was punctuated with him pulling most of the way out and slamming back home. Her body tried to move farther up the bed, but he held her in place. He wasn't ready to leave her heat even if his cock was ready to burst.

"I won't again." Her declaration was made in the heat of the moment as her tight walls clamped around him and had his own release coming faster than he wanted.

His body jerked in time with his twitching cock as he dropped his forehead to hers. Their breaths mingled together.

"I'm going to hold you to that," he told her the moment

he caught his breath. He dropped down onto his forearms and did his best not to crush her much smaller body beneath him. They stayed in that position until his no-longer-hard cock slipped from her body. He watched as their combined juices soaked through his thin sheet.

"We made a mess," Emma chuckled.

"That's because I forgot a damn condom." He hadn't even given it a second thought when he decided he needed to claim her again. He hadn't thought much past the feeling that he needed to show her who she belonged to.

Rolling off of her, he flopped onto his back and threw his arm over his eyes. He really didn't want to have this discussion with his wife. Just the words wife and *are you clean* shouldn't be in the same sentence. Fortunately, Emma didn't seem to have the same problem.

"Well, if you're worried I've been with anyone since I left, then rest assured, sex was the last thing on my mind. I was there for one purpose and finding someone to spend my time with wasn't it."

That wasn't assurance that she didn't have sex; just that she didn't *want* it. Something she said earlier about Armando stuck with him.

"You said you did despicable things so Armando would trust you. Did that include ..." He couldn't even finish the question. He tried. He even opened his mouth like a guppy fish but each time the words got stuck in his throat.

"Ah, no. I don't have the proper parts for what Armando prefers. You would actually be more up his alley than me."

He barked out a laugh before he could stop it. He was never so happy to hear something in his life.

"What about you? Any side flings while your wife was missing? Not that I would be mad, but I'm just curious. Is there a woman out there whose ass I need to kick?"

There was no doubt in his mind that she would, too. Emma was just as possessive as he was. He dropped his arm and turned to look at her.

"No, there's been no one else. Most of the time I was too betrayed by you to want to let another woman in and then it just got comfortable. I used anger and hatred to keep people at arm's length. It worked for the most part. I threw myself into work. Focused on the undercover assignments I had."

Neither of them bothered to get up and clean themselves off. They had the conversation stark naked. At some point, while he was hiding behind his arm, she had stripped her bra off.

"Why did you take this job with Black? Create this team?"

He didn't answer right away. He struggled with that same question now that he knew the truth about her. His initial reason was to find Emma and take out Armando. He hadn't really thought much past that. There was probably a small part that considered walking away, but Black was right. He needed this change.

"I took it because of you. Finding you and Armando was my only priority. That's changed a bit now that I know there is another player and that person also needs to be taken out."

She rolled her lips in. He gave her time to work through whatever questions she had. He expected there were several, and he would answer them the best he could. If he wanted a future with her, then she had to know exactly who he was now.

"Okay. So let's take them. Let's do it together."

He liked the sound of that and he planned to show her just how happy it made him.

CHAPTER EIGHT

Daniel's place was empty. As in, completely empty. A bed and appliances that were probably put in when the place was built were the only things around. She didn't need luxuries, but a table to sit at would be nice or maybe even a couch, so she didn't have to stand while she ate her omelet.

"How is it you don't have a single piece of furniture in this place?"

Emma shoveled another bite into her mouth while she waited for Daniel to answer. When he had carried her in last night, she hadn't cared to look around. She was otherwise preoccupied several times over. But now, in the light of the morning, she could see all that she missed. And boy, was it a lot. If she planned to stay here, then a shopping trip or two was in order.

"I had no need for it. I didn't plan to spend my time lounging around. A place to sleep was all I needed."

That was sad on so many levels. She didn't know what happened to him over the years to make him think he didn't need at least the basic comforts. He mentioned a few things last night, but at some point, they would need to have a conversation about those missed years. She did note that he was no longer using the present tense, so maybe having her back in his life meant he wanted to live a little more.

"At least you thought to get plates and utensils. Hell, even towels. I guess I should be thankful for the small details. Otherwise, this breakfast would be even more awkward than us just standing around to eat."

Daniel stood across from her shirtless, a dusting of gray hair on his chest. She watched the way his biceps flexed each time he took a bite, and it reminded her of the way those same muscles rippled as he went down on her for a second time sometime in the early morning.

"You should stop eye-fucking me unless you plan to follow through with it. And to answer your last statement, that was actually Liam who bought that stuff, not me. You haven't met him yet but he's a bit of a caretaker. He also thought I was living a bit barbarically."

"Huh." She finished chewing her last bite. "I think I'd like to meet this Liam. He sounds like a smart man."

"He is. He's also the only man from the past few years that I asked to join the team with me."

Well, that was an interesting tidbit of information. She figured it was going to take a crowbar to get him to speak about the years they were separated.

"And what about the rest of your team?" she asked casually. "I'm assuming there is more than just the four of you considering how many houses this place has."

Daniel gathered the dishes and walked to the sink without answering her. She waited him out, giving him time to meticulously wash each piece. When she was sure he wouldn't answer her, Daniel turned around and crossed one foot over the other. He leaned against the sink and crossed his arms over his chest, meeting her gaze.

"There are seven of us, including me, but only six live here. Jaxson opted to stay in Texas with his wife, who already works for her own security company, and meets us for any assignments needed. He's not exactly full-time. You've met Gage and Blayd. I've told you about Liam, so that just leaves Chance and Steel. All three are on another assignment and should be back in the next day or two. Maybe sooner with everything we have going on."

Emma wandered around the kitchen. Taking in the emptiness, she tried to imagine Daniel living there. Eating dinner standing up each night. There was no TV, so he didn't lie about only sleeping in the place. It made her wonder what he did during his downtime. Or did he just work all the time? If so, then his life was no better than the one she lived while they were separated.

"Do you plan to stay with the team after Armando and whoever hired him is taken down? That's the whole reason you agreed to work for Black, wasn't it? So what happens after?"

She trailed her finger along the marble countertop. Whoever designed the house did a good job. A little decorating and the place would be gorgeous.

Daniel kicked off the sink and moved toward where she stood across the kitchen. "If you would've asked me that question a couple of days ago, the answer would've been a resounding I don't know. I know you think it's just a suicide mission, but we'll be taking out scumbags. Sure, we'll be getting paid by bigger scumbags, but eventually, their time will come as well."

She wasn't sure she completely agreed with his logic, but he still hadn't answered her first question.

"And now?"

"Now I'm leaning more toward a yes, I'll stay, despite Black's betrayal."

She tipped her head back so she could look into his dark eyes. "And why's that?"

"Because I have a feeling Black pulled you back so you could join my team. And if that's true, then I don't plan to leave."

Most women wanted flowers or jewelry. Not her. She swooned over statements like that.

"And what makes you think I plan to stay? I only chose to work for Black for one reason. And now, after all these years, I'm this"—she brought her two fingers together between them—"close. After that, I could be free and tell Black to shove it."

She was enjoying this; she didn't want to make things too easy for him. She'd already given him her body after less than twenty-four hours. He wasn't getting her heart back that easily.

"You could, but you won't."

"Did you really just growl that response at me?"

He growled right in her ear and it was the hottest fucking thing she ever heard in her long forty-eight years. She wanted to crawl up his body and mount him right here in the kitchen, not caring that she was sore because they spent the entire night reacquainting with each other. She would do it all over again.

"I did. What do you plan to do about it?"

Well, fuck. She wasn't the only one thinking about continuing with their all-night festivities. She was fully on board with whatever plans Daniel had, but before she could answer his challenge, someone was ringing the doorbell.

"I would say saved by the bell, but considering I'm

contemplating murdering whoever is on the other side of that door, it doesn't seem appropriate."

She shoved Daniel back with a laugh. "No murdering anyone today. Not when it's probably one of your teammates."

She strutted to the door and yanked it open without bothering to see who was on the other side.

"I hope you have a very good reason for stopping by. Daniel isn't exactly in the friendliest of moods."

"Is he ever?" Black pushed past her with a smirk.

"What do you want?" Daniel spat.

She looked at her boss as if to give him the *told you so* glare. But Black wasn't the least bit phased.

"An invitation to breakfast would've been nice. Although the lack of furniture would probably have made me decline. When the hell do you plan to make this place livable?"

She tried to hide her smirk, but considering she was saying the same thing not that long ago, the laugh just sort of popped out.

"Never, if it means people will stay away from me."

The death stare that accompanied that statement only made her laugh harder. It had been so long since she was relaxed enough just to enjoy herself. She was going to soak it up for as long as she could.

Black turned to her and pointed a thumb at Daniel. "How do you tolerate this man?"

She gave both her boss and her husband her sweetest smile. "Patience. A whole lot of patience." She figured Daniel understood her double meaning when he glared at her.

Oh, and a lot of love, but no one needed to hear that out loud.

"Why are you here, Black? I was enjoying my morning before you interrupted it."

"I bet you were." Black's hearty laugh had Daniel pinching the bridge of his nose. "Sorry I ruined it, but we have a lead on Armando."

Now the humor was gone.

"You could've led with that!" She threw her hands in the air. She needed to get dressed; she was running around in panties and one of Daniel's shirts.

"And miss out on harassing Daniel?" he laughed. "Yeah, I don't think so. You've got ten minutes to meet the team over in the main building. Make sure you use the time wisely."

Emma didn't waste any time dashing down the hallway to Daniel's bedroom. The only clothes she had were the ones she was captured in. She was in desperate need of new panties and there was no way she could wear the same dress, not after Daniel ripped it in half. There was no salvaging that particular outfit.

"Grab a pair of my sweatpants and a t-shirt. I'll make sure you get clothes today."

Daniel moved in behind her and placed a kiss on her temple. It was in complete contrast to the man he showed the world. Including the man he was around her since he captured her.

"You always knew how to read me better than anyone."

She stayed in his embrace for an extra moment. It was a minute more than she should have. Not because she was weak. At least, that's what she kept telling herself. No, it was because for ten years she'd denied herself the one comfort she needed in hopes of gaining vengeance. And she was tired.

"You're easy to read. At least to me. And only me."

She relished in the possessiveness of his tone. She could be as independent as she wanted with everyone else, but she would always cave to his bossy tone.

"Only to you."

"Get dressed." He kissed her one more time. "We have a murderer to find and a daughter to avenge." He started to walk away, but stopped and added, "Oh, and a boss to annoy since he insists on poking the bear."

She let her laughter follow him out.

CHAPTER NINE

Their New Mexico base of operations wasn't large or fancy. It was nothing compared to what Black had back in Maine, but that was on purpose. Daniel wanted simple. He didn't want the flair or flash of money. He wanted to be so far out in the middle of nowhere that no one would want to come to find them. Black wanted Daniel's team to be a phantom, and he wanted to live as such.

"My intel team back in Maine found Armando thirty miles away from his villa. He's hiding out in a secondary location. I've also sent one of the other teams to look through the wreckage and see what they can salvage. With any luck, some of the information you stashed away survived."

"Set me up with a secure network," Emma replied, "and I might be able to gain some of the knowledge back. Not all of it, since Armando didn't trust technology, but there are still trails, and I made sure to leave myself breadcrumbs to follow over the years."

There was something primitive about having his wife stand in a room full of his teammates talking about taking down a murderer while wearing his clothes. He knew that underneath the rolled-up sweatpants were his boxers. Almost everything that touched her skin smelled of him and that made him want to pound on his fucking chest.

If they weren't trying to find the person who murdered his daughter, he would steal her away and chain her to his bed for the next few weeks, make up for the years they lost together.

"Is this why you refused to take on an analyst for your team?" Black asked him. "You were waiting for the perfect one to come along?"

Daniel didn't bother to answer his boss or the knowing smirk on his face. Black already played his hand with that one, and there was no use rehashing it. There was no way Daniel could've known that his wife wasn't the backstabbing bitch he thought her to be when Black offered him the job. He didn't choose an analyst because he didn't know one that was good enough. Emma set the bar high when they worked together and he couldn't settle for mediocre.

"You can have your analyst discussion after we find out who hired Armando and take them out," Emma interrupted.

He admired her determination because it matched his own. "She's right. We can talk about it later." He turned to Emma. "We have the equipment you need. Feel free to set up in any of the offices. None of us have claimed one yet."

Daniel ignored Emma's strange look. There was no reason to keep explaining that the first assignment he took was hers. That his sole focus, since the moment he agreed to Black's offer, was to find and end her. He hadn't even cared to set up their building. If it weren't for Black's insistence, they would be working out of tents.

"Liam, Steel, and Chance will be back in two hours. We can fly out at nightfall. Have a base of operations together within an hour of that," Gage informed them.

"I'm not sure how much I can find out in that time, but I'll do my best," Emma said. "Last resort, we can torture the information out of Armando. I've dreamed of doing that since I started working for him. Especially after all the hoops he made me jump through."

Daniel's eyes burned a hole in the side of his boss's head until Black turned to look at him. Black slowly shook his head. In no uncertain terms, he let his boss know that the subject wasn't dropped and he would be asking again later about what exactly those hoops were.

"I like the way she thinks," Blayd chuckled.

He needed to have a long conversation with Blayd about the appropriateness of speaking in regard to his wife. That, or he was going to have to schedule a weekly beatdown for the man. He preferred the second option, but figured Black would be opposed to it. New team and all.

HOSTILITY WAS ROLLING off her husband in waves for the last hour. If she had to make an educated guess, she would say it had to do with Blayd's comment. Most would think Daniel had a *don't give a damn* attitude about him, but she knew the truth. He was possessive. The type of over-the-top caveman that would drive a weak woman crazy thinking he was either insecure or didn't trust her. He was neither. He cared deeply for very few people, but the ones he did had his undying devotion. Until they pissed him off. Then he wanted to kill them. Blayd was close, and she needed to distract her husband. Quickly.

"I believe you promised me my own clothes. Any chance of that happening before we fly out?"

She didn't look up from the computer she was feverishly

typing on. She needed to find the information that it took her years to obtain in a matter of hours. Only now she didn't have to worry about Armando figuring out what she was up to. He would know soon enough that his miserable life was over.

"I'll gladly go pick out some clothes for you."

She paused mid-stroke and looked up to find Blayd's dazzling dimple giving her all of its attention.

"While most days I would encourage a good ribbing amongst team members, I can tell you with absolute certainty that you're one comment away from a death sentence." She arched her eyebrow before returning back to her work. "But hey, suit yourself."

The pounding of a fist on flesh didn't surprise her, nor did the grunt that followed. The fact that it only happened once did though. She wasn't the only one getting soft in her old age. The old Daniel would've landed at least two more before Black was forced to pull him off.

"I'll go get those now so you have them before we leave."

She leaned into the brush of Daniel's lips across her hair. All this time, she never realized how much she missed working with him. No promises were made yet, but with any hope, after they handled the Armando situation, Black would allow her to stay on with the team. Emma was more than ready to get back to a life she actually enjoyed living.

The day flew by too quickly. The only time Daniel could convince her to walk away from the computer was to eat and shower. She missed the relaxation of his oversized clothes but it felt good to be back in a pair of cargos and boots. She would give anything to never see another dress or pair of heels again.

By the time night fell, she had only recovered half of the information she needed. The rest would need to come from

Armando himself. She finally met the other team members. She was surprised to learn that Liam was around her age. For some strange reason, she expected everyone but Daniel to be in their late thirties or maybe even early forties.

Steel was just as big as Gage and she learned the two of them worked together previously while in the Army, doing almost the same thing as what they were doing now. She had a million questions about that, but they would have to wait until after the mission. Chance surprised her the most. He looked more businessman than a mercenary. Especially when he walked in wearing a suit and tie. Now that they were on the plane, he was dressed as the rest of the team, in tactical gear.

"The contact we sent to watch over Armando states he is still holed up and hasn't had any visitors. What can you tell us about Armando?"

She looked first at Steel, the man who asked her the question before meeting the gaze of every man on Daniel's team, except for Liam, who was currently flying the plane.

"He's weak and I know how that sounds, but it's true. When I first started working for him, I wasn't sure I had the right man. He doesn't seem like the type of man who would get his hands dirty and kill anyone. He's paranoid and soft. A good lap dog, so to speak."

It was hard to describe a man she both lived with and hated for so long. She spent every day studying him and still she couldn't figure him out. She knew he killed her daughter, had seen the proof in his little black book—yes, he legit had one—along with a dozen other names. Not only had he written down names, but dates and places as well. But she couldn't reconcile him with the person he was behind closed doors.

"Will he go down easy?"

She thought hard about Gage's question. She really didn't know how to answer that, but saying she didn't know wouldn't work.

"Maybe." She lifted her shoulder a bit. "Truthfully, I would be surprised if he fought back. He'll probably break in five minutes."

"So, why didn't you just interrogate him from the start?"

Daniel's accusatory tone put her on edge. He had shown her nothing but softness while she worked, but he was back to the hardened warrior now that they were on the plane.

"Because I needed proof. Yes, I was given Armando's name, but something was off. It wasn't just his demeanor, but the way he safeguarded everything. I knew there was more going on and I didn't think beating the shit out of him would get me the answers I needed, so I chose to see what I could learn. That took a while. Paranoid is an understatement. I don't think any one person in his organization knew what another was doing. He kept everything separate. Not even Black and all his analysts could figure out who was behind things. I needed to keep my cover."

Armando had his hands in everything. Money laundering, racketeering, drugs, prostitution. If it was happening, he knew about it. But that was hard to prove because those under him did all the dirty work. Armando was just the figurehead. Someone else had more power than him and that was who she spent years trying to find, only to come up empty-handed. Because Black pulled her out too soon.

"I wasn't accusing you of anything. I was just wondering what made you stay undercover for so long. An assignment that long changes people."

It did change her, but not in the bad ways Daniel thought.

"It made me stronger. Made me realize that I'm so much stronger than I thought. There were days that I wanted nothing more than to kill him slowly, but I realized whoever Armando worked for had to be more powerful, and I didn't want to leave the loose end open, so I learned patience."

A hard lesson learned. One she thought she would fail a million times while living in that villa. Every time Armando challenged her to prove her loyalty. Every depraved thing she was forced to look at while doing his books. Several times she wanted to just end his life, but then she remembered why she was there. Kali deserved better.

"Now you have a team at your back and we can torture him for the information. We can finally stop things."

The rest of the plane ride was spent discussing strategy. A team this large wasn't needed to restrain one man, but there was no way of knowing if whoever hired Armando would have provided him protection. Gage felt it wasn't likely based on their informant's report, but Black refused to allow just a couple of them on the assignment.

When it was time for them to land, she could feel the anger rolling off Daniel. Just like her, he was ready for it to be over. Ten years was a long time to avenge the death of their daughter.

"One step closer." She grabbed his hand and intertwined their fingers. And it was in that same position that they walked off the plane. Unified again in their shared cause.

CHAPTER TEN

It was in the dark of night that his team moved in unison to the secondary location where Armando was hiding; a house much smaller and older than the villa Armando was used to.

"I don't show any guards on the perimeter," Chance told the team over comms.

Chance and Emma were nestled on higher ground and provided them with coverage as they moved closer to their target.

"Anyone else think it's strange that he doesn't have any protection?" Gage mirrored his own thoughts.

Daniel asked himself that same thing a dozen times since landing. All reports showed that Armando was alone and unprotected, and while that was what the initial intel gave them before he took Emma, he still felt it weird. Wouldn't someone be providing Armando protection after he fled?

"The dynamic between Armando and whoever hired him has never made sense to me," Emma replied. "Just one of the many things that kept me there for so long. Protection never seemed to be a major concern for him."

"It's time we ask him. We move on three."

He counted down in his head, just like his team. By the time he hit one, he was moving through the brush and stopping at the front door. Liam was on his left. Gage and Steel took up the rear door and Blayd would move in once Chance and Emma came down from the hill.

Liam nodded and slammed his foot through the door. Wood splintered as the door crashed back against the wall. He moved in high, Liam low. A similar commotion echoed from the back of the property.

They cleared the first room and found Armando trying to make a run for it in the second room. Dropping his rifle and letting the sling catch it, Daniel charged and tackled Armando to the ground. Daniel flipped him over and straddled the man's waist. With a quick three-jab combo to the jaw, Armando's head slumped to the side.

"Find me something to tie this asshole up with."

He stood guard over an unconscious Armando while Liam went to find ties. The other members of the team checked in as they cleared the rest of the house and surrounding property. Just as they suspected, no one was sent to protect Armando. Whoever the man worked for clearly didn't value their employee very much.

When Liam came back with rope, he helped his teammate haul a heavy and still-knocked-out Armando into a chair and tied his hands behind his back and his legs to the chair. There would be no way for him to escape.

"Do you have a picture of Kali?" Daniel asked.

Emma walked up next to him. He had one he always carried with him, but it was worn and barely recognizable anymore. Emma already confirmed their daughter's name was amongst others on a list, but he needed to hear it for himself.

"Here you go. I asked Black for a fresh picture before we left."

Leave it to his wife to always anticipate what he would ask for.

"Some things never change." Daniel's lips turned up into the smallest smile, the first he'd had on a mission in a very long time.

"I was both married to you and worked with you for a while before Kali's death. I know what you are going to ask before you even think about it," she laughed.

He took the time to laugh with her. It was morbid considering he was about to torture a man for information, but that was their life and it wasn't going to change. Not while working for Black, and Daniel had a pretty good idea Emma would be staying on with his team.

"Time to see what this asshole has to say."

Liam tossed a bucket of water over Armando's head until the man woke up sputtering and spitting it out. Daniel watched as he looked around frantically, trying to figure out what was going on. But it wasn't until his eyes landed on Emma that his expression changed.

"Emilia?" Armando attempted to pull at his restraints. "What the fuck are you doing here, and who are these men?"

Daniel had to control the urge to wipe his wife's name from the man's mouth, even if it was only her undercover name. His wife could handle herself and she wouldn't thank him for stepping in on her behalf.

"It's Emma, actually, and these men are with me." He raised an eyebrow at her. "Okay, more like I'm with them but that's not important. But you know what is important?

You giving us some information. Information I spent way too many years trying to find on my own."

Daniel stepped in front of Emma and threw a punch to the man's jaw, snapping Armando's head to the side.

"That's for speaking to my wife the way you did. I suggest you remember that for the rest of this conversation." He patted Armando's cheek and pulled out the picture of his daughter.

"Remember her?" He shoved the picture in Armando's face. "You killed her. Were *hired* to kill her. Now it's time to pay for that sin."

Armando's face drained of all of its color. His whole body started to shake just from one glance.

"No." He shook his head back and forth like he was possessed.

Well, that answer just wasn't going to work.

"No, you don't remember her, or no, you weren't responsible for her murder? And before you think of lying to me, I have it on good authority that you were the man who pulled the trigger. Really good authority."

He didn't let the fear that he had the wrong man show. That one word had him questioning everything the CIA told him when it happened. They weren't exactly known for their honesty.

"Yes." Armando's voice shook. "I killed her, but he made me."

Now they were getting somewhere. Even if that somewhere was a whining bitch in front of him.

"Who made you?"

Armando tried shaking his head again in denial, but Daniel's fist struck out and stopped the movement, causing the man to tip back in his chair and crash to the floor. Daniel was on him before Armando could scream out, his fists raining down over and over. Hitting not just his face but his ribs and stomach as well. All of the years of frustration poured out of him.

"That's." A punch. "Not." Another punch. "How." An elbow to the face. "This." A knee to the ribs. "Works."

He would've kept going, but two sets of strong hands were hauling him off their hostage before he could continue.

"You can't kill him yet," Steel snapped. "We need a name first."

He struggled against Steel's iron grip, but it was no use. Like Gage, Steel was a powerhouse of muscle.

"Daniel!" Emma got into his face and pushed her body so it was completely flush with his. "Rein that temper back in. It's not the time to lose it. We need him alive and that can't happen if you beat him to death, so settle the fuck down!"

That pulled him from whatever rabbit hole he fell down. He'd waited so long to get his hands on the man who killed his daughter that he should've realized he would lose himself.

He should step away and let someone else handle the interrogation, but he wouldn't. It needed to be him.

"I'm good."

He shook off Steel's loose grip and paced the small room. His team kept an eye on him and he watched as Liam picked up the chair with Armando still attached. Both were put back into a righted position.

Liam woke Armando up again. Once everyone was sure Daniel wouldn't kill him, he was allowed back to his interrogation.

"Let's try this again. You said someone made you. How about you tell me what you meant by that?"

He didn't lay a finger on Armando. He didn't have to. The man looked terrified and ready to spill his guts. Being knocked unconscious not once, but twice, probably had something to do with it.

"He made me kill her. He made me kill all of them," Armando whined. "It was either kill them or he would kill me."

"So you chose your miserable life over that of a little girl? An innocent little girl who did nothing but make everyone around her smile."

Now the anger was back and Daniel had to restrain himself once again.

"I never asked why he wanted me to kill the people he ordered me to. I just did what he wanted so I wouldn't die. Going against him was never an option. He wouldn't let me."

Pathetic.

"And?"

"And what?!" Armando screeched.

Seriously? The guy really thought he was just going to take that explanation and be okay with it? Daniel wanted to roll his eyes at how absurd that was, but he settled for something better.

"Tell me who you work for."

He slammed his fist into Armando's face. The sound of bone crunching gave him perverse satisfaction. So did the dribble of blood that leaked from the asshole's mouth and eye. There wasn't a spot on the man's face that didn't look like it had been put through the wringer.

"Vito Accardo!"

The man actually blubbered the answer like a baby. He was an absolute disgrace, but the name he gave them rang a bell.

"The don of the Italian Mafia?" Liam asked.

"Yes." Armando was full-on crying now. It was pitiful to know that this was the same man who killed his daughter. Daniel would've thought only a hardened killer could take the innocent life of a child. Armando was proving that was false.

"Where can we find him?"

Daniel threw another punch, this time into the man's ribs. Not because it was needed. No, Armando now seemed eager to share what he knew. But he needed to take out some of the pent-up rage and what better way than on the man in front of him?

"I don't know." Armando cried out when Daniel's fist connected with his other set of ribs. "He just asked me to meet him here and guard his investment until he could get back. The boss doesn't exactly share details and to ask would mean death. I just did as I was told."

"Funny. Seems your boss and I have something in common." Daniel could see the confusion in Armando's bloody eyes. "We both plan to kill you."

When Armando still looked confused, Daniel explained further. "If you really think Vito didn't plan to kill you when your usefulness ran out, then you're a bigger idiot than I thought."

"I'm telling you the truth," Armando begged. Blood dribbled down his chin and stained the no longer perfectly pressed shirt.

"Oh, I believe you. A man like Vito Accardo would never tell someone so weak such sensitive information, but now I'm more curious about this investment he had you guarding. What is it and where? Tell me and I'll make your death quick and relatively painless."

Relatively was a loose term. The man was already

feeling the pain that he and Emma had suffered for the last ten years.

"I don't know." Daniel pulled his fist back, but Armando rushed on. "I swear I don't. The boss wasn't here when I showed up and I haven't heard from him since. I don't even know if what he was talking about is in this place. I know nothing!" he screamed.

Daniel was inclined to believe him. The man was too scared to lie. He might've pulled the trigger that killed Kali but it was done from a distance and Daniel believed the man when he said he had no choice. It was either kill his daughter or die himself. Too bad the man chose wrong.

He pulled the gun from his holster and put a bullet in Armando's forehead before he could even register it was happening.

"Search every inch of the place. I want to know what investment Armando was talking about," he ordered his team.

Liam, Gage, Steel, and Blayd fanned out. Chance stayed to deal with the body and Emma approached him.

"A bullet to the brain was too generous."

Daniel looked back at the man who was still tied to the chair. His face was torn up from the numerous punches he received. Piss stained his tan chino pants and blood dotted his button-up shirt. Armando may have deserved more of a beating, but the man died feeling fear, and that was good enough for him.

"Maybe, but I had no desire to spend more time with the coward." He looked back at his wife. "Besides, it didn't take much to make him piss himself. I wasn't aiming for him to shit his pants as well. That's a smell I didn't want to deal with."

Emma laughed. "Fair enough. I'm sure he wasn't far off.

I always knew he was a weak bastard, but I just thought it was an act so people didn't see the real monster beneath. Now I know he really was just that pathetic."

"I think I found something." Gage's voice traveled through his comm. "I've got a secret door hidden in the downstairs bedroom. It's locked. I'm going to break it down."

"I'm on my way to you," Steel chimed in.

While he waited for his team to report back in, Daniel looked at Emma.

"Are you okay after finding out who was behind Kali's death?"

He looked her over. She seemed to be handling things fine, but Vito Accardo wasn't some small-time criminal. Taking the man on was going to be a big job for Blackguard Security.

"It's not ideal, but I always knew it had to be someone big if it was so hard for me and Black's analysts to find. It sucks we don't know why, but now we have a name and something to go off of."

He smiled at her response. She admitted what he wanted without his prompting or even asking.

"I see that smirk, and yes, I plan to stay with the team, but you already knew that, so don't deny it. We were a great pair, so why stop now?"

Why stop indeed? They were a perfect team, and they had years to make up for. He leaned down and placed a quick brush of his lips across hers. She was lucky there was a dead guy in the room or he would've tried for more.

Even as he was contemplating that thought, Gage came over his comm.

"We have another problem."

EPILOGUE

Steel

He followed Gage's directions to a secret door at the back of the house. A secret door in a closet in a bedroom. Cliché. Steel cleared rooms again on his pass. They took down Armando, but his boss wasn't in the house as they expected. Daniel and Emma were pissed. Understandably. They'd waited years to get the person who murdered their daughter, and Armando was only half of that. The other half was the head of the Italian Mafia and someone that would be hard to take down.

The broken lock on the floor made his blood boil.

A woman. Vito's so-called investment was a woman locked in the basement.

Who the fuck thought it was okay to lock a human being up in a basement? Just when Steel thought he had seen it all, there were assholes like Vito who proved him wrong.

Steel descended the steps slowly. Gage was already

down there, but he would never assume all threats were eliminated.

The smell of urine, feces, and a hint of blood had him holding his breath. To force someone to live in those conditions was despicable. He took a quick moment to sweep his flashlight around and take the small room in. A dirty mattress sat in one corner where Gage was kneeling down in a non-threatening manner, trying to calm whoever was held hostage. An overflowing dirty bucket stood just ten feet away. The more he took in, the angrier he got. The room was nothing more than a concrete slab with exposed pipes and cement block walls. Only one very small barred window let in even the barest sliver of moonlight.

Steel lowered his weapon and moved in Gage's direction. Two more steps and his flashlight allowed him to get his first look at the person sitting on the bed.

"Karlie?" Her gaze snapped up at his choked question.

Barely three feet in front of him was the woman he had spent the last eleven months looking for after she suddenly disappeared.

They'd had one glorious weekend together and promised that they would stay in touch. But he had gone back to the Army and she had ghosted him. So he spent every resource he had trying to find her. He'd taken the job with Blackguard Security because they were supposed to be the best at finding people. But all his efforts had been for naught. Until now.

The room was silent as he looked her over. His heart broke all over again with each bruise and cut he noticed. The sheer amount of dirt and grime that covered her face and hair. But he wasn't prepared for the sound that finally broke the silence.

A baby crying.

Want to find out why Karlie went missing? Don't miss Steel and Karlie's story in Reclaiming What's Mine.

WHERE TO FIND ME

Interested in staying in touch?

I love connecting with my readers.
For sneak peeks, teasers, and a fun community
please join [Elizabella's Ladies Reader Group](#)
or follow me on [Instagram](#), [TikTok](#), [Goodreads](#), and
[Bookbub](#).

ACKNOWLEDGMENTS

Thank you, Amanda Sisco-Willett for helping me name our Female Main Character. As an author, it gets hard trying to come up with names for so many people, so again, thank you!

ALSO BY ELIZABELLA BAKER

Charlie Team Series:

Ashlynn's Savior

Leah's Warrior

Zack's Redemption

Missy's Champion

Jaime's Vengeance

Bentley's Forever (novella)

Heroes of Lone Star Series:

Fighting for Charlotte

Burning for Chloe

Caring for Lucy

Arguing for Alexa

Bravo Team Series:

Protecting Ember

Chasing Trista

Guarding Jewels

Hunting Kendra

Securing Abigail

Harboring Shantae

Deserving Maddie

Stand-Alone:

Westley

Blackguard Security: Phantom:

Crossing Enemy Lines (prequel)

Reclaiming What's Mine

Made in the USA
Monee, IL
19 April 2025